Duck
has a day out

Illustrated by Peter Lawson
Series editor: Teresa Wilson

Published in Great Britain in 2002 by Egmont Books Limited,
239 Kensington High Street, London, W8 6SA
Printed in Italy
ISBN 0 7498 5486 3

10 9 8 7 6 5 4 3 2 1

Educational consultant: Betty Root, formerly Director of the Reading Centre in the University of Reading.

"Hello Duck," said Bridget,
The Fat Controller's granddaughter.

"No, I'm not Duck, I'm Percy,"
said Percy.

"Oh, sorry," she laughed.

Duck and Percy were working in the yard moving trucks.

Bridget thought they looked the same.

One day, Percy had to go back
to the station.

"Sorry, Duck," he said.
"I'll come back as soon as I can."

Duck said goodbye to him.

Bridget went to the yard and asked, "Where's Duck?"

"I'm here," said Duck. "It's Percy who has gone back to the station."

"Oh, sorry Duck," she laughed.

Duck had to work hard
now that Percy had gone.

The trucks were hard to pull.

"I hope Percy will come back
soon," he said.

The next day, the driver took Duck
into the country to pick up
The Fat Controller.

His car had broken down.

"I like it here," said Duck. "It's quiet."

13

Percy was in the yard when they got back.

"He's come to help again," said The Fat Controller to Duck.

"Now you can have a day off for working so hard."

Duck's driver took him back into the country.

It was quiet, and Duck was happy just to look at the birds and the bees and the flowers.

"Oh," said Duck, "there's a bee on my nose!"

"Don't move," said the driver.

"But it tickles," said Duck. He shut his eyes and the bee flew away.

"Are you all right, Duck?" asked the driver.

"No. The bee has stung me on my nose," said Duck.

Back in the yard, The Fat Controller put a yellow bandage on Duck's nose.

Percy tried not to laugh.

All the drivers came to look at Duck's nose, and his yellow bandage.

"Does it hurt?" they asked.

"Yes, it hurts a lot," he said.

Bridget came to the yard to say hello to the two engines.

She never knew which was which.

The Fat Controller took her hand and said, "I'll show you."

23

"That one is Percy, and the one with the yellow beak is Duck!" he laughed.

Look at the big
black hat.

1

A duck is in the

big black hat.

I am a duck.

Look at me.

A hen is in the big black hat.

I am a hen.

Look at me.

A kitten is in the

big black hat.

I am a kitten.

Look at me.

Oh! The big black
hat is a trick hat.